New Dog in Town

by Gail Herman
illustrated by John Nez

Kane Press, Inc.
New York

Library of Congress Cataloging-in-Publication Data

Herman, Gail, 1959-
  New dog in town / by Gail Herman ; illustrated by John Nez.
     p. cm. — (Social studies connects)
  "Culture - grades: K-2."
  Summary: With help from his dog Scout, Nick explores his new neighborhood and makes some
friends.
  ISBN 1-57565-165-3 (alk. paper)
  [1. Neighborhood—Fiction. 2. Moving, Household—Fiction. 3. Dogs—Fiction.] I. Nez, John A.,
ill. II. Title. III. Series.
  PZ7.H4315New 2006
  [Fic]—dc22
                          2005021197

10 9 8 7 6 5 4 3 2 1

First published in the United States of America in 2006 by Kane Press, Inc.
Printed in Hong Kong.

Social Studies Connects is a trademark of Kane Press, Inc.

Book Design: Edward Miller

www.kanepress.com

"Nick, do me a favor," Mom says.

"Sure," I tell her. "What?"

"Leave."

We moved yesterday and Mom's freaking out.

"I'll get more done that way," she explains. "You and Scout go explore the neighborhood. I'll even give you spending money."

Sounds good to me!

Woof! Woof!

"Wait up, Scout!" I call. "This isn't like our old neighborhood. You need a leash now."

Lots of things are different here. Houses are closer together. There are more cars. More people. More everything! I hope I get to like it.

At least Scout is the same. He picks up the newspaper just like he did where we used to live.

This is Scout's best trick. He can carry a newspaper, or a slipper—or anything. And he only lets go when I ask.

"Give it to me, boy," I say. I hand the newspaper over to Mom.

A **neighborhood** is a place where people live. It's a small part of a community.

"Hi!" says the mail carrier. "Are you new here?"

"Yup," I tell her. "We just moved in."

"Welcome to the neighborhood." She smiles. "I hope your dog doesn't chase mail carriers!"

"Nope," I reply. "Scout only chases chickens."

"I guess I'm safe, then. No chickens around here!"

She seems nice. I feel a little better about this new place.

Woof! Woof! Woof!

"Okay, boy. Let's get going." Scout and I head for Main Street.

We pass my new school. Two boys are kicking a soccer ball around the field.

Scout wants to play, but I feel too shy to stop.

When people look for a new home, they check the neighborhood. Where is the school? Is there a library? Is there a church, synagogue, or mosque? Are there stores nearby?

"Hey! A Mighty Burger!" I say.

Scout sniffs the air. I tug on his leash and we keep walking. There's lots to see.

We pass a market, a firehouse, and a bank. Some kids are selling plants at a sidewalk stand.

Help keep our neighborhood green!

People can work together to make their neighborhood a better place to live.

Next to the bank is a bookstore. It's bigger than the one in our old neighborhood.

"Wow!" I say to Scout. "They've already got *Goblin Squad #5!* Let's go buy it."

Every neighborhood is different. This one has lots of stores and businesses.

I go up to a man with a tag on his shirt. It says, Ray Garcia, Manager.

"Hi! I'm looking for *Goblin Squad #5*."

"You can't bring that dog in here," he tells me.

"Gee," I say. "In our old neighborhood—"

"Sorry. No dogs allowed. It's a store rule."

"Oh! I didn't know." I back out the door.

Now what? I really want that book.

"Guess you'll have to wait here, Scout." I tie the leash around a pole. "I'll be right back."

Scout gives his tail a little wag.

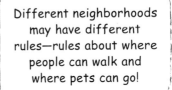

Different neighborhoods may have different rules—rules about where people can walk and where pets can go!

I'm heading for the New Books section when I hear *Ah-whooo!* Some dog must be in trouble.

"Excuse me, young man." It's Mr. Garcia. "Will you do something about your noisy dog?"

"That can't be *my* dog," I tell him. "Scout doesn't howl."

Mr. Garcia points out the window.

It *is* Scout!

I rush outside. "Sorry, Scout! I didn't know you'd be sad."

I'd never tied Scout up before. I never had to—until we moved here.

"Let's keep going," I say. "I'll get the book later."

We've gone half a block when Scout lifts his head. His nose quivers. I smell it, too. Pizza!

Scout skids to a stop in front of Joe's Pizza Place.

"All right!" I say. "Pizza for me and crust for you." Then I see the sign. No Dogs Allowed.

I let out a sigh.

"Okay, Scout," I say. "I need to tie you up again—just for a minute. If you're quiet, we'll both have pizza!" Scout looks nervous.

I take a step and then another.

AH-WHOOOO!

So much for getting pizza.

We pass the library. There's a No Dogs Allowed sign on the grass. There's one in the park, too.

Scout's walking more slowly now, and his tail is down. I feel glum myself. Scout isn't allowed anywhere I want to go.

A library is open to everyone in a neighborhood. What other places do neighbors share?

We walk a few blocks and turn down another
street. There's a huge poster of dogs—all kinds of
dogs—in a store window.

"I bet they'll let us in here, Scout!"

Wrong again.

"Too bad you're not a movie star," I tell
Scout. "They'd let us in if you were Lassie."

Scout just looks at me and sneezes.

There's nothing to do but go home.

Scout barks hello, and Mom gives us a "back-so-soon?" look. I want to ask her to go to the bookstore with me. But she's talking to the plumber and the cable guy.

"Quiet, boy," I say, and we head up to my room.

When people need a plumber, a painter, a carpenter, or other help, they usually call a business in their neighborhood.

I open the boxes and start putting stuff away—
my radio, my globe, my Snazzy Jazzy marker set
and wipe-off board.

Scout nudges me with his wet nose and barks
again. "Quiet, boy. Hold this."

He takes the board in his mouth.

Moving day
June 10th

The wipe-off board has writing on it. It looks like Scout is begging me to read it.

I start to laugh. Then I remember all those signs on Main Street.

"Scout! I think you've solved our problem!"

We hurry to the bookstore. "Hold this, boy,"
I say. Scout takes the board and wags his tail.

"Good dog!" I tie the leash to the pole and go
inside to buy *Goblin Squad #5*. I don't hear the
tiniest woof from Scout.

My plan is working. He can't howl—not with
the board in his mouth!

When I leave the store, Mr. Garcia is right behind me. He sees the sign and smiles.

Two girls stop. "Cute dog!" says one.

"Cute sign!" says the other. "Let's go in."

Mr. Garcia pats Scout's head. "Come back anytime!" he tells us.

I write a new message on the board and we're off to the video store.

Scout holds his sign and doesn't make a sound.
People crowd around and smile.
Some of them go into the store.

Violet, the owner, rushes out with a camera.
"May I take your dog's picture?" she asks.

"Sure," I say. "His name is Scout."

"Hi, Scout," she says. "I'm going to hang your
picture in the window. You'll be a star!"

Scout's a big hit at the pizza place. Lots of people stop—and buy pizza. I see one of the kids who was playing soccer this morning. He has a dog, too!

"Hi, I'm Al," he says.

"I'm Nick, and this is Scout," I tell him.

"Buster and I are on our way to the dog run," Al says.

"Dog run? What's that?" I ask.

"It's a special part of the park for all the neighborhood dogs," Al tells me. "Come on, I'll show you!"

Joe, the pizza man, hurries out. "Business is booming, thanks to you," he says. "Have some pizza—my treat."

The dog run is cool!

I let Scout off his leash, and he dashes over to the other dogs.

Sometimes neighbors get to be friends!

"Scout's having a great time!" Al says.

"He sure is," I say. "I've never seen him so happy—not even chasing chickens!"

That night Mom and I sit down on our brand-new couch. Scout crawls onto my lap.

"Did you have a good day, Nick?" Mom asks.

"I got a new book," I tell her. "And free pizza! And I even made a new friend."

"Wonderful, honey! How was Scout's day?"
Scout lets out a big snore, and Mom laughs.

"That's a long story," I tell her. "At first nobody seemed to want him around. But now Scout's the most popular dog in the neighborhood!"

Welcome to the Neighborhood

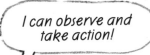

MAKING CONNECTIONS

When Nick explores his new neighborhood he observes No Dogs Allowed signs everywhere he looks! So he trudges back home—where a great idea spurs him into action. . . .

Just like Nick, you can observe all day long. But if you want to start making changes—in your class, your school, or your neighborhood—you have to *take action!*

Look Back

- What does Nick observe in his new neighborhood? What can you observe in the picture on pages 8–9?
- On page 21, what is Nick's idea? How do you think he comes up with it? Does his plan work? Why?
- Look at the pages where Nick and Scout visit Violet's Video, Joe's Pizza Place, and the dog run. How does taking action change the way Nick feels about his new neighborhood?

Try This!

Take a walk around your school with a friend. What do you observe? Is there anything that could be improved? Would signs help? What would they say?

Take action! Make a list of signs you'd like to see in your school. Make sure you get permission before you put them up!